Deena's Lucky Penny

by Barbara deRubertis
Illustrated by Joan Holub and Cynthia Fisher

The Kane Press
New York

Book Design/Art Direction: Roberta Pressel

Library of Congress Cataloging-in-Publication Data

DeRubertis, Barbara.
    Deena's lucky penny/by Barbara deRubertis; illustrated by Joan Holub and Cynthia Fisher.
      p. cm. — (Math matters.)
    Summary: While pondering how to buy her mother a birthday present
with no money, Deena finds a penny and follows a process of discovery
about how pennies add up to nickels, which add up to dimes, all the
way up to four quarters making a dollar.
      ISBN 1-57565-091-6 (pbk. : alk. paper)
      [1. Money—Fiction. 2. Birthdays—Fiction.] I. Holub, Joan, ill. II. Fisher, Cynthia ill.
  III. Title. IV. Series.
PZ7.D4475De 1999
[E]—dc21   98-51117
                                                         CIP
                                                             AC

10 9 8 7 6 5 4 3 2 1

First published in the United States of America in 1999 by The Kane Press.
Printed in Hong Kong.

MATH MATTERS is a trademark of The Kane Press.

Deena had a problem—a big problem. Her mom's birthday was coming. But Deena didn't have any money to buy a present.

Not one penny.

Just then Deena saw something shiny in the grass. A penny! She picked it up. The penny felt warm in her hand. "Wow!" she said.

"What's up, Deena?" called Mrs. Green from next door.

"Look what I found!" Deena said.

"Oh! A lucky penny!" said Mrs. Green.
"Do you know this rhyme, Deena?"

Find a penny.

Pick it up.

All the day you'll have good luck.

"How can a penny be lucky?" asked Deena.

"I'll show you," said Mrs. Green. She pulled a handful of coins out of her pocket. "I'll give you four more pennies to go with your penny. How much money do you have now?"

"1, 2, 3, 4, 5 cents," said Deena. "That's the same as a nickel. Thanks, Mrs. Green!"

"Which would you rather have?" asked Mrs. Green. "Five pennies or a nickel?"

"A nickel, please!" said Deena. She traded Mrs. Green the five pennies for a nickel.

"Hey, Deena!" a voice called.

1¢ + 1¢ + 1¢ + 1¢ + 1¢ = 5¢

It was her brother, Sam, pedaling back from his paper route.

"Look, Sam! I found a lucky penny," Deena said. "Mrs. Green gave me four more pennies. Then she traded me a nickel for the pennies."

"That *was* a lucky penny!" Sam said. "What are you going to do with your five cents?"

"Save it," Deena said. "Mom's birthday is next week. I need money to buy a present."

"I'll give you another nickel to go with that one." Sam pulled a nickel out of his pocket. "Now how much money do you have?"

"5 cents plus 5 cents equals 10 cents," said Deena. "That's the same as a dime! Thank you, Sam."

"Which would you rather have?" asked Sam. "Two nickels or one dime?"

"A dime," said Deena.

They traded coins.

"It's funny," she said. "A dime is much smaller than a nickel, but it's worth more!"

"Twice as much!" said Sam.

5¢ + 5¢ = 10¢

Deena's big sister Amy skated up to Deena.

"Listen, Amy," Deena said. "First I found a lucky penny. Then I got a nickel. And now I have a dime! I'm going to buy a present for Mom's birthday."

Amy smiled. "That dime looks lonely," she said. "I'd better give you another one."

20¢

"Thanks, Amy!" said Deena. "Now I have 10 cents plus 10 cents. That equals 20 cents. I'm going to show Dad!"

10¢ + 10¢ = 20¢

"Look, Dad! I found a lucky penny—and now I have two dimes!" Deena said. "I'm going to buy a present for Mom's birthday."

Dad reached into his pocket. "Here's a nickel to go with your two dimes. How much money do you have now?"

25¢

"20 cents plus 5 cents equals 25 cents," said Deena. "That's the same as a quarter!"

"Would you like to trade your two dimes and one nickel for this quarter?" asked Dad.

"Yes! Thanks, Dad!" said Deena.

10¢ + 10¢ + 5¢ = 25¢

Deena could hardly wait to show her quarter to Grandma and Grandpa. They were coming for supper.

Deena set the table.

She stacked her books.

She changed her clothes.

Finally, she heard the doorbell.

"Grandma! Grandpa!" Deena said. "I found a lucky penny—and now I have a quarter!"

"Wow!" said Grandpa. "How did that happen?"

"Like this," Deena said. "I found a lucky penny. Mrs. Green turned it into a nickel. Sam turned it into a dime. Amy turned it into two dimes. And Dad turned them into a quarter!"

"What are you going to do with your
quarter?" asked Grandpa.

"I'm saving it to buy a present for Mom's
birthday," answered Deena.

"Then you may need more than twenty-
five cents," said Grandpa. "Why don't I give
you another quarter?"

"Thanks, Grandpa!" Deena said.
"25 cents plus 25 cents equals 50 cents!
That's half of a dollar!"

25¢ + 25¢ = 50¢

"Deena," Grandma said, "Will you let me try a magic trick with your two quarters?"

A magic trick? With her two quarters? Deena wasn't sure. But then she saw the twinkle in Grandma's eyes.

"Okay, Grandma," said Deena. "But please don't lose my fifty cents!"

Grandma took the two quarters. She dropped them down into her big purse. "Abracadabra!" said Grandma. She waved her hand over the purse.

21

Then Grandma reached down deep inside
her purse. Slowly, she pulled out her hand.

"Four quarters!" Deena cried.

First, Grandma put three quarters in
Deena's hand.

"Now let's see how much money you have," Grandma said.

"25 cents plus 25 cents plus 25 cents equals 75 cents," said Deena.

$$25¢ + 25¢ + 25¢ = 75¢$$

Then Grandma put the last quarter in Deena's hand.

"75 cents plus 25 cents equals 100 cents," said Deena. "And 100 cents equals ONE DOLLAR!"

She gave her grandma a big hug.

"Would you like to trade your four quarters for a dollar bill?" asked Grandma.

"Yes, please!" said Deena. "Now do I have enough money to buy Mom a present?"

"Yes, you do," said Grandma. "Tomorrow I'll take you to the Dollar Store. They have lots of things for a dollar."

25¢ + 25¢ + 25¢ + 25¢ = $1.00

By now dinner was ready. Dad peeked around the kitchen door. "I think I hear Mom coming," he said.

Sure enough, Mom walked in.

"Mom! Guess what?" Deena said. "I found
lucky penny today!"

"Lucky you!" said Mom. "What are you
going to do with it?"

Deena couldn't help smiling. "It's a secret,"
she said.

That night Deena thought about her lucky penny and how it grew from a penny to a dollar...from one cent to one hundred cents.

It was just like Mrs. Green's rhyme.

Find a penny.

Pick it up.

All the day you'll have good luck.

Today had been a *very* lucky day. And tomorrow would be even better. Tomorrow she would buy her mom a birthday present!

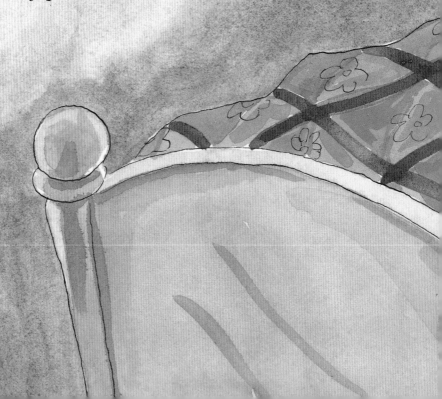

Money Chart

penny	nickel	dime	quarter	dollar
1 cent	5 cents	10 cents	25 cents	100 cents
1¢	5¢	10¢	25¢	100¢ or $1.0

Here are two ways to make each amount.
Can you think of other ways?

5¢	5 cents	1 nickel	5 pennies
10¢	 10 cents	2 nickels	1 nickel, 5 pen
20¢	 20 cents	2 dimes	1 dime, 2 nicke
25¢	25 cents	2 dimes, 1 nickel	5 nickels
50¢	50 cents	2 quarters	5 dimes
100¢	 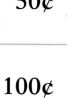 100 cents	4 quarters	8 dimes, 4 nick

32